A Walk On The Other Side

Other Side

Erotic Poetry

The Quiet Poet

A Walk on the Other Side

A Walk on the Other Side

COPYRIGHT ©2014 Ernestine Wright

Printed in the United States of America

ISBN-13:978-1500364151
ISBN-10:1500364150

Printed by Createspace 2014

Published by BlaqRayn Publishing 2014

A Walk on the Other Side

"If time is the master of fate for all of mankind... I just want us to be in the same space in time at the right time to create our own moment in time that will be everlasting...

Not for for anyone else but just for us. Because you and I are love !!!"

The Quiet Poet

A Walk on the Other Side

A Walk On The Other Side

The Quiet Poet

Dedication

This book is being dedicated to someone who is very special to me. Davey Lee Zeigler, you left us much too soon. You will be missed more than I can ever say. My love for you is everlasting and may you forever rest in heaven with the Father, loving you always my cousin, my brother, my best friend. Without you there would not have been a S.P.R.E.A.D.!

4/30/1966-6/5/2014

A Walk on the Other Side

Acknowledgment

My mother Frankie Wright, you carried me, now you encourage me and I thank you and love you more each day of my life.

To my children Darnell, Janell and Tamesia, love you all always even though you all said I was being grown, But you still told me to continue writing what I felt.

To my father Edward Wright, my best friend thanks always and forever for all our talks you always know what to say to make me feel better, my other Mom Joyce Carter-Wright, I'm singing you are my friend.....

Darlene Wright my sister, my rock you are always in my corner never saying much, but always there thank you and my love is your love always !!!

A Walk on the Other Side

My Big Brother, Johnny I hope this has earned me a " Platinum Card " Loving You

My Sissy Michelle you already know, you and together to the end of time nothing can separate our love !!!

Rene Ransdell, The Best Manager, thank you for believing in me, for being my friend, my ear, my shoulder to cry on, praying with me; basically just being you. Now that we have embarked on this new journey I know God is going to continue to bless us because at the beginning of each day He comes first, and you have seen the best in me through Him.

Thank you my friend.

Another Place

There are two parts of love, one when we fall in love and the other when we fall out of love... I don't want to experience either I just want to go to another level with you, another realm, another place, far beyond our imagination…past the center of the abyss of sensual pleasure.

There we will discover a new world that others have dreamed about and talked about. So now it's our time just take my hand as we begin this journey to another place where there is nothing but extreme pleasure awaiting us.

CHOCOLATE KISSES

Chocolate kisses is what comes
to mind when I look at you.
Nice sweet and so delicate
chocolate wrapped up in a nice
package. Yes it's a small
package, but when you reach
me,there is a part of me that has
been yearning for just a taste of
your chocolate kisses, goes into
shock at your touch.

My mind and my body go into
a complete different realm and
there is not a soul there except
you and I and you and your
chocolate kisses. Just in a
moments time I embrace you
into my spirit and we become
one and now I know what it
feels like to be a chocolate kiss.
I am warm, all of senses are

A Walk on the Other Side

sharp and my spirit has left my body. I feel like electric shocks are going all through my body, all of this come from just one of your chocolate kisses. I want to stop, yet I refuse to let go, I want to come down from my high, but it feels so good, so I guess I will say here where I am just me and my chocolate kisses.

DO YOU WANNA DANCE

I live my life listening to the rhythm of the words in my mind that creates the poetry I write and read then share with you ...

The words come and I start to feel the beat and and I start to move and and my hips start to sway and I feel like dancing and I can't contain myself!!!! I feel like I'm floating far beyond the heavens and yes what a feeling and I only want a one way ticket...

The mood is just right and so who on this beautiful day that we have been blessed want to

A Walk on the Other Side

dance with me...Remember my dance is about words and feelings coming from within my soul and I'm floating so high in my spirit right now and I looked down and my feet haven't left the ground. Now, I say that's some shit, it's cool, because it feels so good it has to be right and if you don't want to dance with me I'm still good!!!!

Because this dance I'm doing is so dam amazing I tell you because the wind just blew up my dress and I'm feeling just right, like when the Isley Brothers sang Summer Breeze make me feel fine my, my, my I feel good I'm singing Happy right now while I'm dancing...

A Walk on the Other Side

So, I ask you do you want to
dance with me, if not carry
on   my loves and I will see you
on the next time the wind
blows...

FEED ME

I was so hungry, but food wasn't on
my mind... When I think of you I just
get hungry and I need to be fed. I'm
on fire and calling 911 is not the
answer. I'm just hungry and I need to
be fed...there is no way that I can
continue to keep going until I get fed
by you.
You see, others have offered to feed
me in your absence, but you have
that Midas touch.
Just at the thought of your skin
touching mine, awakens fiber in my
body that has been
dormant to the point that my body
starts to release juices as if you
where here with me.

I have yearned for this moment for
you and I to occupy the same space
and time so we can tap into a new
place of sensual awareness   that is
awaiting us,all I ask is that you feed
me and feed me until I can't take
anymore.

A Walk on the Other Side

As you begin to explore my body, I start to shiver with anticipation. Your tongue is arousing every sensual feeling in my body. You began kissing me and talking to me and telling me exactly what you where going to do to me, and my body starts to release my juices even before you enter just from the way you expressed your desires about feeding me and missing me.

I was so ready and my body arched as you entered and I tried to scream but nothing came out ...I tightened myself around your thick and juicy shaft to let you know you had made it home and you have been missed...once again   I wanted to scream and nothing came out but how good it felt to be getting fed and my hunger was slowly going away...

I had to make sure your hunger was taken care of as you pulled out and then with a long thrust you re-entered and I let a scream that

A Walk on the Other Side

would have awaken the angels on the
other side of heaven... We where
almost at that point, but it was time
to go for a ride I so gently climbed
on top and slowly slide down on that
beautiful thick now sticky shaft
while I held your hands to ensure I
was able to take all of you,   then
slowly I turned around and grabbed
your feet and   and rode your
wonderful, thick and juicy, shaft
until it was covered in my juices.
Has I looked over my shoulder I
could see the look of total and
complete satisfaction on your face
which pleased me even more.

At this point I turned around slowly
making sure that you and I where
still connected and kissed you gently
and thanked you for feeding me in
my time of need.

HOME WITH HIM

I ran, yes I ran until I couldn't run anymore. As I ran I could feel the grass beneath my feet and the wind was racing through my hair and all I could think about was getting home to you. It had been a long day and it was Friday and the rain was coming down and that's was all that was on my mind was getting home to you.

The sun was shinning but the rain was coming down in buckets and I was getting soaked and yet all I could think about was getting home to you. Mary who lived around the corner stopped and said "girl get in this car" I replied "naw girl I'm fine enjoying the rain", but I was thinking about my man and how he was going to hold me and love me and caress me all night long and there was no room for her because all I was thinking about was how I was getting home to you.

A Walk on the Other Side

My sweet chocolate thunder, my chocolate "prince" My everything that treats me just right like no other who makes my insides leap and jump with just a touch or just a word on occasion because he is my man and has I walked through the rain all I could think of was how I was going to get home to him. Finally I reached the door and there he stood looking as fine as ever, holding a towel just for me, so you know how the story ends. I knew what was next as he assisted me in getting out of those wet clothes now that I was home with him.

Intoxicated

Your love is so very intoxicating, and with every breathe I take it becomes even more intoxicating...So on today I choose to be drunk, because love won't let me wait. Yes, I can't wait to breath again...to get that feeling of complete drunkenness as I breath in your sweet essence .

You don't even need to be near me your essence is forever in me, on me, around me, you are always in my thoughts, you are in my soul, in my spirit you and I are connected. I feel you coming before you get here and I'm anticipating what an amazing and electrifying encounter we are about to enjoy.

There are no words to explain what is about to happen, just silence and pure natural, beautiful unadulterated   no holding back I

belong totally to you, sweat
dripping from head to toe
sex!!!!!!   Then we breathe and
once again I'm totally drunk,
intoxicated and so very happy
basking in the moment knowing
that this is just the beginning...

You are intoxicating to every fiber
of my being, you are that good
feeling that's so dam good that you
should be illegal. What you are
doing to me is a crime, but when
they try to lock you up for this
crime of extreme passion, I will
testify that it was I that allowed you
to cause this damage to my
midsection, because it felt so dam
good.

They will probably say that I'm
drunk and out of my mind, which is
true because being around you, I'm
in a constant state of drunkenness,
you are intoxicating to my soul and
yes I choose to remain drunk as I

A Walk on the Other Side

breathe the essence of your love
and drink your forbidden drink that
I can't get enough of...I just ask one
thing of you, just continue to fill
me up daily and keep me
intoxicated with your love...

IT'S TIME

I have never touched those smooth chocolate lips of yours that often appear in my mind. I often think of you and your chocolate skin and how it would feel against my body as we experience moments of undying passion. I have waited what seems like a lifetime for this moment. This has been my dream for a very long time. Then that day finally comes and I get to feel your lips on my lips and I get to feel your skin on my skin and, my body is just about at the breaking point and we have just gotten started. Then suddenly were are there and you ask me to wait, but I can't. I'm trying so hard to contain myself and keep my love from exploding all over you, but it's so very hard, since I have been waiting what seems like a lifetime for this moment, a dream I have played over and over in my mind a thousand times, and now it's here and I'm about to just loose my mind and go

A Walk on the Other Side

into a place where I have never been before, a place that lovers have talked about and I have only dreamed about. He must have sensed my excitement as he kissed my neck and I moan and my body is moving as if he had already entered my doorway to heaven. He looked at me and smile and said" in time baby girl, in time". At this point I could no longer speak, because if I did, I think the only thing that would come out would be "just might take me right now", so I just smiled back at him. I want so bad for you to touch me and kiss me all over , but I can't speak, or is it that I won't speak, or is that I'm scared to speak because I just don't want this feeling to end. Once again he must have sensed my feelings because without warning he took my breast in his mouth and he gently caressed the other one with his hand and I entered another realm of pleasure as he continued making love to my breast and then he switched to make sure they received equal attention. My body was just about at the point of no return when suddenly I felt his manhood grow even more and I just didn't understand that. As I grasp for air and he chuckled as if he knew what was going through my mind. All I could think was all of that was for me, and my body started aching even more. Then without warning I felt his manhood leave my leg where it was resting and it felt so good while I massaged him. As he placed his manhood inside of me, ever so gently I knew I was not going to be able to hold my love back it was going to come down like a waterfall, but oh how I tried, I wanted this moment to last as long as possible. This was the moment of truth he was inside of me and I was in another world, and everything was perfect in my world so perfect that a tear formed in the corner of my eye and rolled down my cheek. He looked at me and asked me "are you ok,"? Once again, I could not speak because I was in paradise. I looked at him and smiled and shook my head yes as my body arched to meet him each time. Then it happened I was going to explode and he knew it because I arched my body so he could go as deep as possible and he said " baby please wait" I could barely catch my breath because all my love had come down at one time, I had finally reached that place far beyond the heavens. The only thing I had to say was oh baby, excuse me while I kiss the sky.

OH LA LA LA LA

Oh la la la la la la is what I begin to
sing as the time gets closer and
closer to the time when I get to be in
your arms again. That feeling of total
completion is all I long for. My days
have   been so long and my nights
have been longer since the last time
you held me ever so tight within
your warm embrace. Oh la la la la is
all that I can say each and every time
I'm with you, only because there are
no words to describe the way you
make me feel, I just go oh la la la la
la...I can't explain what happens
when I'm with you...it feels like the
heavens open up and pull us in as if
we are floating on a cloud of pure
and unleashed love that as taken over
and we have no control of the heights
that we are about to reach... How I
look so forward to reaching those
heights with you...

As I take your hand I begin to feel as
if the earth is no longer beneath my
feel and I'm walking on clouds and
my sensual journey as begun and
once again I look at you and words
escape me thus the only thing that
comes out is oh, la, la, la, la as we go
higher and higher all you and I have
is the heavens and heights that that
we are striving to reach. Once again
all I can say is oh la la la la la only
because there are no words to
express the feeling of total
satisfaction that I experience when I
am with you. You have reached
down I'm my soul and parked your
everlasting love for me there and oh,
how I so enjoy the feeling complete
submissiveness as you enter into my
soul and once again I can say nothing
but oh la la la la la la la...

Right now I want to scream, that
silent scream for I have reached the
point of ultimate stimulating ecstasy
with you and I am once again falling
and I need you to catch me, in your

A Walk on the Other Side

arms where I long to be, where I
need to be ....as I say oh la la la.   I
reach out to you, as you reach for me
and the space between us is growing
smaller and my body simply aches
for you and I shall not resist the
pleasure that you give me, so I will
say oh, la la, la, as we begin to climb
once again to this ultimate high
which is being in your arms and
receiving all the love that you have
to give me, until I pass out from
complete sexual exhaustion ...saying
oh la la la la la la la la la

Love Me

You want me, then love me,
look at me... see me in all of
my beauty...see me in all of
glory...just love me...Can you
handle me...don't tease
me...for I will please
you...only if you can love
me...and I mean all of
me...Leaving nothing to my
imagination, yet taking to me
places that I never been
before...

I can see the heavens, they are
within my reach, but you take
me to another place with one
touch...Just another tease,
when all I want you to do is
please me, for I please you...so
I ask one last time, do you

A Walk on the Other Side

want me, then love me, and
simply just come and love all
of me...

MY MAN

I want my man to love me like never before... I want my man to hold me tight and let me know I'm all he will ever need, I need my man to just love me like there is no tomorrow... I need

I need my man to love me until I can't tell whose sweat is covering my body, his or mine...I just need my man to love me like we are running out of time and we only have tonight and tomorrow doesn't exist...I just want my man to love me, hell I promise you I will love you back until you go limp and get up again....

I will love you until the sun rises against the morning dew and we won't smell anything but the sweet essence of our love making that consumes the air we breath...yes I will love you until the end of time and let you start time again so we can keep this thing going over and over and over again because there is no end to the ways that I can dream of to love all of you...one night is not enough, a day is just a tease, we need a time machine to stop time so that we can have enough time to explore every inch, every area of sensual pleasure and make sure we reach the fullest extent of pleasure that is expected...no we need to exceed all expected pleasures principals before moving on...

This is why I need my man to love me and yes I promise to love you back slowly and completely and repeating it all until you are satisfied beyond anything you ever dreamed of...so are you ready to be my man and are you ready to love me...because I'm so ready to love you!!!

My Tears

My eyes are bright and full of life... My heart is full of happiness when I'm with you... Your touch sends me into a place I can't describe but if you look into my eyes you will see the tears that are falling from my eyes but I'm far from sad...

These are the tears of passion, for I can't speak to express the feelings of complete and total satisfaction that you give me.

My tears are uncontrollable because your touch sends me in so many different directions, if I tried to speak it would be in a foreign tongue...you are my afternoon delight that turns into my evening meal, that quickly becomes my midnight

A Walk on the Other Side

snack...and you are my morning glory that sends me to a point of no return and that's when my tears speak for me.

NO MORE MILES

Giving oneself over and over again, looking searching for that one person that will fill that empty void has found itself to be a search that is turning into something that is much bigger that I ever expected.

It all starts with a phone call then we meet after that the long awaited kiss that sometimes sends me into another world and sometimes I just have to dismiss myself from the scene, only because a kiss is worth a thousand words and if I can't find one word to say after a kiss, then I'm sure there will be nothing else for us to talk about or engage in at a later date.

Now if that kiss is worth the wait, then we shall in time move on too other things, but me and my hot ass has a problem waiting !!! Especially if he is tall an little thick and

A Walk on the Other Side

chocolate and help me good Jesus if he is bald... I'm done another one bites the dust and here we have logged some more pussy miles... We are not trying to log any pussy miles right now, because that's only a temporary fix and right now we need a permanent solution to this problem. We need to fill this void without accumulating anymore pussy miles.

Okay, it's a new day and I have got to fill this void, Mom says wait on God... Dad says yes He is all that you will ever need, but Poppy says yes Mommy I love it when you make me feel like that !!! Now dayuum , I just can't go down that street again... I have to put the brakes on and make a U-Turn, because my mileage indicator is about ready to rack up a few more miles today. Now, we wash her, shave her, make her, smell nice and fresh and sometimes she needs to go for a ride...But today is a new day and my motto today is no more miles, that is pussy miles ...

A Walk on the Other Side

because I need to fill this void.

Here we go again... This is the date I have been waiting for...Mr. Pecan Tan and so fine, but I will keep my tank locked and engine off and we are in park. The music is nice, the room is mellow, the food is great and the company is awesome!!! We danced and and I felt something that made me want to turn that dam key, and let's get this party started and get into to overdrive but I was good as hell, I'm so proud of me. We sat and talked about what we wanted and where we wanted this relationship to go...

Ladies. it is a wonderful thing when you run across a man with the same issues as you !!!Trying to fill a void, not wanting to jump into bed, just wanting to take it slow... It's great. We kissed good night and we looked at each other and yes it was one of those kisses that could have gotten me in a lot of trouble. As we parted, I

did see a change in formation so to
speak and it was a beautiful sight.
We both looked at each other and
said no more miles...Right now..

PERFECT FIT

My life is now at a point where I consider it to be full and complete since you have come into my life, for a long time I have existed on my journey thinking I was complete, but now I see and feel what I have been missing and it's a wonderful feeling.

Your smile brightens my entire day, your touch sends me so high that I have reached   the point where I have seen the back gate of heaven and I didn't even know that existed. When you touch me my entire body trembles and shakes as if I was having uncontrollable seizures, but it's just that good down home loving that you give me each time touch me. Just think I thought I was complete, who the hell was I kidding besides myself.

Ok, I'm coming down from a natural high or should I say my man's high

A Walk on the Other Side

and still feel good. Yes baby, now it's that time when you just tap me on the shoulder and I just wiggle over just a little and snuggle right in the curve of your sexy body. Yes, this is where I want to be...This is a perfect fit, and even though we just came back from the other side of heaven, laying here in your arms and feeling that wonderful, now that beautiful and tasty piece of meat growing behind me is exciting me so that I'm ready to go for another ride, but you are already sleep and I'm left alone with my thoughts and a hard dick dayuum what's a girl to do??? I know I need to use what I have to get where I want to be again....Did I say tasty...

Role Playing

AS I WALKED ACROSS THE
ROOM I COULD FEEL HIS EYES
ON ME, THEY FELT LIKE
BURNING FLAMES GOING
THROUGH MY SOUL. I
COULDN'T COMPLAIN
BECAUSE IT WAS NO HOTTER
THAN THE FEELINGS THAT I
HAVE FOR HIM, THAT I WAS
TRYING SO HARD TO HIDE AS I
WALKED AND DID EVERY
THING I KNEW HOW NOT TO
ACKNOWLEDGE HIM. THIS
WAS INCONCEIVABLE SINCE
HE WAS TALL, PECAN TAN
AND OH, SO FINE. HIS
SHOULDERS WERE STRONG
AND WIDE, HIS ARMS WERE
LONG AND MUSCULAR, HIS
LEGS WERE LONG AND LEAN
AND HIS EYES ARE A PERFECT
LIGHT BROWN AND HIS SMILE
LITE UP AN ENTIRE ROOM, SO

A Walk on the Other Side

TELL ME HOW YOU CAN WALK
PASS THIS MAN AND NOT
LOOK HIM, BUT THAT IS THE
WAY HE WANTS TO PLAY
TONIGHT. AS I CONTINUED TO
WALK ACROSS THE ROOM, I
MADE SURE THAT I SWAYED
MY HIPS JUST A LITTLE MORE,
AS I SMILED AT ANOTHER
MAN THAT WAS CLEARLY
INTERESTED IN SEEING WHAT I
HAD TO OFFER... I FINALLY
REACHED THE OTHER SIDE OF
THE ROOM AND SUDDENLY I
FELT A HAND SLIDING
AROUND MY WAIST THAT
GENERATED SUCH A BURST OF
ENERGY THROUGH OUT MY
BODY THAT I ALMOST LET
OUT A SCREAM OF EXTREME
PASSION, BUT ONCE AGAIN I
HAD TO CONTAIN MYSELF.
BEFORE I COULD SAY
ANYTHING I FELT THE
WARMTH OF HIS BREATH ON
MY NECK AS HE BEGAN TO
SPEAK IN MY EAR "YOU LOOK

A Walk on the Other Side

SO BEAUTIFUL TONIGHT" MY
HEART WAS RACING AND MY
BODY WAS FEELING LIKE IT
WANTED TO RELEASE EVERY
OUNCE OF LOVE THAT I HAD, I
JUST WANTED TO EXPLODE AS
HIS WARM BREATH
SATURATED MY BEING. THE
MUSIC STARTED AND I
COULDN'T RESIST THE
SOUNDS AND THE VIBRATIONS
AND MY HIPS STARTED TO
MOVE AND SWAY IN WAYS
THEY HAD NEVER MOVED
BEFORE. WITH HIS HAND STILL
AROUND MY WAIST, HE
BEGAN TO FOLLOW ME AND
WE DANCED, AS IF WE WERE
IN OUR OWN WORLD. IT FELT
LIKE I WAS IN A TRANCE AS
WE DANCED AND DANCED AS
IF IT WERE A LIFETIME AWAY.
AS WE DANCED SO CLOSE TO
EACH OTHER I FELT HIS
MANHOOD RISE TO THE
OCCASION. AT THAT POINT I
WAS READY TO JUST LET GO,

A Walk on the Other Side

YET WE WERE NOT ALONE. AS
WE CONTINUED TO DANCE IN
OUR OWN TRANCE, I FELT
MYSELF WISHING THAT THE
SONG WOULD GO ON FOREVER.
BEFORE I KNEW IT HE GENTLY
KISSED ME ON MY NECK, AND
AT THAT POINT MY BODY
COULD NOT TAKE IT
ANYMORE. I EXPLODED
WITHOUT HIM BEING INSIDE
OF ME. I COULD NOT CONTAIN
MYSELF ANY LONGER. I LET A
MOAN OF SATISFACTION THAT
ONLY HE COULD HEAR, AND
HE WAS PLEASED. THEN
WITHOUT WARNING THE
MUSIC ENDED AND WE HAD
NO CHOICE BUT TO COME OUT
OF OUR TRANCE, NEVER
WANTING TO LET GO. HE TOOK
MY HAND AND I FOLLOWED
WITH A SMILE BECAUSE I
KNEW IT WAS TIME TO GO TO
THE OTHER SIDE.

SENSUAL JOURNEY

TEACH ME, SHOW ME... MAKE
ME SCREAM...I WANT TO
TOUCH THAT CLOUD THAT IS
BEYOND THE MOON...THAT I
HAVE NEVER BEEN TOO...JUST
LOVE ME GENTLY, SO THAT I
WILL HUNGER FOR YOUR
TOUCH EVEN WHEN YOU ARE
NOT HERE, WHEN YOU ARE
WITHIN MY SIGHT MY BODY
WILL START TO CLIMB YEARN
JUST FOR OUR TOUCH AND MY
INSIDES WILL BE BURNING AT
THE THOUGHT OF YOU
TOUCHING ME ONCE
AGAIN....IT'S LIKE A VOLCANO
ABOUT TO ERUPT AND I DON'T
WANT TO MISS A MOMENT OF
THIS WONDERFUL RIDE WE
ARE ABOUT TO EMBARK
ON...JUST YOU AND I AND THE
PASSION THAT IS INSIDE OF US.
YOU HAVE IGNITED A FIRE

A Walk on the Other Side

INSIDE OF ME THAT ONLY YOU
CAN EXTINGUISH...DON'T
MAKE ME WAIT TO TAKE THIS
JOURNEY, FOR IF WE DON'T
GET STARTED SOON, I MIGHT
HAVE TO SATISFY MYSELF
WITHOUT YOU, WHICH WILL
ONLY TAKE ME HALF WAY TO
THE HEAVENS THAT I LONG TO
REACH ONCE AGAIN WITH
YOU. OH HOW I LONG FOR
YOUR TOUCH, THE WAY YOU
MAKE LOVE TO MY BREAST
THE WAY YOU SO GENTLY USE
YOUR TONGUE TO AROUSE MY
BODY AS YOU TEASE ME
WHILE TASTING EVERY PART
OF ME LEAVING NOTHING TO
MY IMAGINATION. FOR I CAN'T
THINK STRAIGHT WHEN I'M
WITH YOU, THE ONLY THING
ON MY MIND IS HOW LONG
WILL IT TAKE US TO
REACH   HEAVENS OF
SENSUAL   BLISS WHERE I
WILL LET GO OF THIS SEA OF
LOVE THAT I HAVE BEEN

A Walk on the Other Side

HOLDING ONTO JUST FOR YOU.
MY MOMENT HAS
ARRIVED...HERE WE ARE , THE
JOURNEY HAS BEGUN, YOU
HAVE YOU JUST TAKEN MY
BREAST IN YOUR MOUTH AND
YOU ARE CARESSING THE
OTHER AND I AM STARING TO
FEEL THE FIRE WITHIN
ME   GETTING STARTED AS
YOU GENTLY TAKE YOUR
HAND AND SLIDE IT DOWN MY
BODY AND SEPARATE MY
LEGS SO THAT CAN PLAY
WITH ME AND DRIVE ME ME
CRAZY...WITH ONE HAND YOU
ARE TEASING MY CLIT, AND
WITH THE OTHER YOU HAVE
TAKEN A FINGER AND
INSERTED IT INSIDE ME JUST
TO MAKE SURE I WAS WET
AND ENJOYING YOUR
ATTENTION...I SO ENJOYED
THIS PART ONLY YOU COULD
ALWAYS FIND MY SPOT AS
YOU WOULD WHISPER IN MY
EAR IS THIS MY "G-SPOT

A Walk on the Other Side

BABY !!!!" MY BODY FEELS
LIKE ITS DANCING ON A
CLOUD AS YOU INSERT
ANOTHER FINGER AND MY
BODY ARCHES TO   TO
RECEIVE ALL THAT YOU ARE
GIVING TO ME...MY BODY IS
ON FIRE, AND I FEEL LIKE I
WANT TO EXPLODE AND YOU
TELL ME TO WAIT...AS YOU
FLIP MY BODY OVER AND
BEFORE I KNEW IT I FELT YOU
ENTER MY BODY WITH ONE
GENTLE STROKE AND I LET
OUT A SCREAM OF PASSION
THAT I'M SURE THE GATES OF
HEAVEN HEARD AND THEY
OPENED UP TO AWAIT OUR
ARRIVAL...JUST AS I WAS
ABOUT TO RELEASE MY SEA
OF LOVE YOU ONCE AGAIN
ASKED ME TO WAIT AND YOU
TURNED ME BACK OVER AND
RE-ENTERED MY BODY WITH
ONE LONG THRUST THAT FELT
SO GOOD I COULD NOT
SCREAM, BUT A TEAR FELL

A Walk on the Other Side

FROM MY EYE, THUS A SIGN
OF TOTAL SATISFACTION. AS
YOU CONTINUED TO LOVE ME
LIKE NO OTHER I COULD NOT
HOLD ON ANY LONGER AND
WITHOUT WARNING MY SEA
OF LOVE EXPLODED AND IT
WAS LIKE WE WERE LOST AT
SEA AND THE SHIP WAS
ABOUT TO HIT LAND, AND OUR
SCREAMS OF PASSION ECHOED
AROUND US AND THE GATES
ARE OPEN AND THEY
ACCEPTED US FOR WE HAVE
JUST COMPLETED ANOTHER
SENSUAL JOURNEY...

SHHHHHH

Shhhhh,I just saw him...walking toward me...my man, my love... My lawd was this the man that has promised to love me eternally, unconditionally, without any questions...Well dam....I'm speechless, my heart is pounding more like racing should I stay should I run...Damn...for once I who always have words of wisdom, love and much more have nothing to say...as he reached me there were no words to be said as he swept me up in his arms for that wonderful, breathtaking, lip smacking oh my lawd help me I'm so weak if he wasn't holding me in his arms I would fall, make you want to just strip first-time kiss. ..

Wow, can I say wow again...What a kiss, I still standing and I'm still trying to hold on. I have just been to the other side of the heaven and back again and that was just with a kiss...

A Walk on the Other Side

Oh my, the anticipation of what's
coming next has me leaping with joy,
for finally I will reach the mountain
top with him, yes with who I have
dreamed about and longed for.

Now our moment has arrived, the
moment of inception when the two
of us have become one...That
glorious moment when we came
together and our bodies locked and
for an instant time stopped and we
where actually one. The heavens
opened up and the angels sang a song,
not to mention the song my body
was singing...The juices leaving my
body at this moment will put the Nile
River to shame has Cleopatra herself
sailed across, because this Queen is
truly honoring her King, so I say to
you shhhhhhh I have no more to say
for the River is flowing...

A Walk on the Other Side

S.P.R.E.A.D

As we sat embracing and enjoying the moments of warms kisses and gentle touches my heart began to race even more longing for you to be inside of me more than ever before. But for some unknown reason you have kept me waiting for what I have been longing for what seems like forever. Then suddenly you whispered in my ear would I be interested in a spread? Not knowing what it was, but willing to please my man I quickly said yes. With that you took my had and led me to the bed and so very gently laid me down, then spread my legs and spread my legs so he could have a full view of my vagina as he took a quick taste then smiled and began to tell me what this SPREAD was all about; SUPER PUSSY RIDING ENORMOUS ASS DICK. Wow, need I say anymore...

A night to remember

A Walk on the Other Side

MY TELEPHONE LOVER

My day has ended and I laid in my
bed thinking of you and then like
clock work the phone rings, and my
heart begins to race and I can't wait
to hear what you have in store for me
tonight. As I pick up the phone my
heart is racing with so much
anticipation, for I know that with
your words alone you will take me to
places that only lovers have gone. I
said hello and when you spoke I felt
a release in my soul that made my
whole entire day disappear. Your
breathing on the phone was hot and
heavy and I closed my eyes and
imaged you laying with me, inside of
me I felt your breath saturating my
entire being and I began to become
even more aroused. Then you asked
me was I ready and I answered yes, I
reached down and inserted our
substitute into my warm and over
excited body as you talked me
through the entire experience. What

A Walk on the Other Side

a ride I was on as I reached the top of
the clouds you knew it was time and
you allowed me to reach out touch
the heavens and explode all at once.
As I began to catch my breath I
heard your voice in the distance
saying baby, I'll be home soon. I was
still speechless because I had just
had another round with my telephone
lover.

THAT PICTURE

Clearly since meeting me you have
not learned or saw anything would
have made you think the size of
your penis would excite me into
communicating with you on that
level before time. FYI... It is not the
size of your penis that would
interest me... It's the size of your
brain and what's inside of it and
what will comes out !!!

Can you hold a conversation, can
you relate to me one on one other
than in a nonsexual manner, can
you respect me, do you want to
know all of me the uninhibited
me...the natural sweet me, the me
that will bear her soul and share all
of her secrets with you, the me that
saw you standing on stage doing
your thing and putting it down and
said said dam now that that brother

A Walk on the Other Side

of another color is doing his
thing...The me that sat up all night
in the coffee shop listening to you
talk about your dreams...

Now we have crossed another line
a first kiss and still we have not
decided to be intimate because of
pass hurts...I'm still the me that sat
up and watched you while you slept
and wondered what you are
dreaming about and hoped that it's
me because if we have reached that
point because we where heading in
the right direction so why in the
fuck would you ruin what we had
by sending me a picture of your
half erected penis...

Clearly my dear it was not the size
of your penis that had me it was
you but now you can show your
penis to the next woman, because
I'm me and my dreams are
important and clearly you don't
know me if you think the size of

A Walk on the Other Side

your penis would have made me jump... So I say to you I will jump, I will jump back into me and my dreams and fly high and you can come watch me put it down like I do...

THE AWAKENING

Allow me the honor of saying good
morning to you my love.. I must
say you have awakened in me
something's that I thought where
sleep and would never wake up
again and for that I just want to say
thank you.

Let me just stand over here and
look at you as the sun comes
through the window and gazes
upon your beautiful black skin, yes
I'll just stand over here and talk too
you because boy you have done
something to me and right now I
could eat you up for breakfast, but I
have yours cooking on the stove
right now.

I just want too, I just want too you
see you got me so confused I can't
think right. I just can't put into
words how you made me feel last
night. It was like I was floating on a

A Walk on the Other Side

cloud and you just kept taking me
higher and higher until I couldn't
breathe and I was begging you too
stop and you looked at me and said
are you sure and me with my hot
ass said no give me more...Hell, it
was like you had me hypnotized
but baby it was more like you had
me DICKMATIZED. Yes I can
admit it, because when it feels that
good I gotta let you know.

Yes, yes, oh yes, look at you
smiling at me like that, no I can't
come over there right now I just
want to continue to sit here and
look at you as the morning dew
settles on the peddles of Gods
beautiful flowers outside this
window, and smell the flowers that
have bloomed as we made love
while the sun was coming up...and
look at me one might say I'm in
love, maybe but I will tell you this
after you have your breakfast and I
have mine I do plan on tasting you

A Walk on the Other Side

for lunch... Yes , baby today is your
day like I say you have awakened
in me things I can't even talk about
but I will show you all day.

Guess what, I have a special treat
for you, yes I do after all is said and
done today... No..I I think I might
let you wait awhile, because you
have toyed with me and played
with me oh and yes how about
when I finally reached my peak and
started to release you did something
to me I never experienced before,
my body shook from head to toe
and I felt a sudden flash of heat and
I just screamed because it felt so
dayuum good and all you did was
smile.

It's ok my love because I have been
talking to you telling you what's in
store for you today because there
will be no phone calls for help, just
you and I because you have
awakened the freak in me and

A Walk on the Other Side

today is the day that I will eat you
for breakfast, taste you for lunch
and swallow you for dinner. Oh,
FYI this process will be repeated
daily until you realize who is in
charge, and now who really loves
you !!!

The Cloud

Sometimes when I think of you my mind just goes so high and so far I just keep floating into a land that's so beautiful it's no miracle that I don't want to come back. What we have when we are together is a blessing like no other. The way you make me feel is like, I'm on a cloud and I have floated far above the heavens and it's just you and I and the air is clear and you reach up and grab a star and place it on the cloud and the light shines ever so brightly, because of the passion and love that we share.

As we float through the heavens you touch me and my body starts to quiver and that's only because I have been waiting or so long....You touch me again and I moan, your touches are like music to my soul a song that I will play over and over again for I can never get enough of you !!! As you continue to touch me I don't want to wait for you and my body is

A Walk on the Other Side

yearning and wanting you so bad that
I am already releasing my juices and
you have not even entered my body,
you have only just kissed by neck it's
just your touch and I have just been
waiting for you for so very long...
Just the thought of you inside me
right now is making me want to
scream, but I will wait until the
moment is right because I want to
reach that moment with you and only
you, that's why I have been waiting...

With each kiss you keep taking me
higher and higher and this cloud is
amazing it has changed shapes and
positions to hold us because you
have moved my body in so many
different ways as you kiss my body,
tease my body, caress my body, you
have just done all kind of wonderful
things to my body, yet you have not
entered my body...

I felt it this wonderful cloud that we
are on just went up a little higher and
now I don't know if it's what your are

doing to me or if it's how high we are that I can't catch my breath either way I love the way I'm feeling right now !!!! I want to scream but I can't, I want to tell you stop but I won't dare, I want to tell you I want more but I'm scared, I want to tell you I love you but what will you say, oh my I just want to call your name but nothing comes out..

Then it happened I felt you enter my body oh my, I tried once again to scream but nothing came out.... One long thrust and I was ready to pass out.. How long I have waited for this this was the feeling of complete ecstasy a feeling of being completely one with you !!!! We continued to make loved and oh my the feeling of you going in and out of me is something that I can't put I into words but I know one thing when that last last thrust came has you took my leg and placed it on your shoulder knew what was about to happen...

A Walk on the Other Side

With a long gentle thrust you entered
in me all the way so that you could
make sure I was completely yours
and I would know no other man
could take your place within me...
Before I could say anything I
couldn't hold it any longer and
neither could you it was like the
heavens shook and we both let
screams of passion that even shook
the gates of heaven...Was I satisfied
oh yes, and where you satisfied I
would say so...But for some reason
neither one of us where able to speak
yet, so we just cuddled and floated
on our cloud waiting to start all over
again...

A Walk on the Other Side

THE FIRST TIME

Your love as me feeling like I have
fallen into an abyss of pure and
sensual pleasure.
When I close my eyes I feel like I'm
floating on cloud that has gone so
high, and I have Surpassed the
heavens and oh my it feels so good,
Is there a way I can stay here forever.
Yes, forever in a state of sensual
pleasure,
All of this has happened, you have
yet to Enter my body with one long
gentle thrust
That I long for, my body is aching
and yearning To go higher and
higher, yet you are insisting on
making me wait to go to another
level, oh how I screamed out loud as
passion took my mind, body
and soul. I have just entered another
realm of of pleasure
and yet you have not entered my
body. You smiled at me
knowing what I want, yet you are
making me wait, within that moment
I could not hold on any longer my
body exploded my juices came down
like a water fall and you responded
what took you so long. I gave you

A Walk on the Other Side

what you wanted, so I was ready to receive you as my body arched to let you enter and you were warm and long just like I dreamed you would be. I had no idea what was going on, but I felt like I was spinning on that cloud for a moment then I fell and there I was falling again into the abyss of sensual pleasure, but I was not alone you were with me and we both reached that point of undying passion at the same time and our bodies were one intertwined in love juices that were flowing like never before and be both let out screams of passions that left an echo in the air that I wished I could still hear, we were in another realm, another place, we made love for the very first time...

THE NATURE OF THE BEAST

Let me explain. The nature of the beast...Fucking is and essential part of a relationship let that be known and like another woman, I love to be fucked because it feels good to be dipped, flipped, and slapped on the ass a few times...

Then there comes the time when the lights are low and the mood is right and we must take our time and do things slowly so that the moment will last...You see, what we need to do is be creative and create a space just for two...So that we can make sweet uninhibited love without boundaries so that when it's done my body will be glowing under the the moonlight has it glistens in the beauty of the afterglow of the because the sweat that has been left on my body from yours...

A Walk on the Other Side

Yes, that's pure, unadulterated good love making sweat that comes from the nature of the beast within you and me...I just want you to make it rain on me, and I promise to make it rain on you, hell let's make a storm...Trust me it's Nature Of The Beast!!!

The Unmasking

You have unmasked, what was inside of me and released this untamed beast that has an insatiable desire to devour you until my appetite can be satisfied. The feelings I experience when I'm with you are ones of true ecstasy, higher points of sexual heights that I have ever been too before. The Heavens even look strange for this height !!!

When I'm with you I experience feelings that I have never felt before, you have truly unleashed this beast inside of me. This beast that has been laying dormant for years, untouched, not being treated right, not being loved the right way, not being caressed, kissed, licked, sucked the way I should until you..set me free.

From the first glance, that first look that went through me like a warm sensation that had my juices flowing.

A Walk on the Other Side

Yes, this was all new to me until you came I to my life. Your unmasking of the beast within me has caused a shift in the wind which has caused a shift in the atmosphere and I have no control over what happens next...

All I know is I'm in constant anticipation waiting upon more of your continued unmasking of this beast inside of me... Each moment, each touch, each second is always a memory to me captured in time never to be forgotten by me. You are the keeper of this beast, my submission is purely and completely electrifying in every aspect. I look forward to more heightened ecstasy as you continue unmasking the beast within me.

The Whisper

It was new, it was nice no it was beautiful yes that's it...the most beautiful feeling that I have ever experienced with you. This shocked me, I mean it really shocked me. Right at this moment I was actually stuck, frozen time I couldn't move, nor could I say a word. I was in total disbelief. I could not even explain what I was feeling even if I were to tell someone right now. What you have done to me; you have placed me in another place and time, its like I fallen into an abyss and I'm not sure of sensual pleasure and I have come out on the other side and it has placed me on a completely different realm pleasure and I have never been here before and I don't want to come down. I just want to stay right here and bask in the sweetness of the moment that you have created just for me. This is that moment that every woman dreams of when she

A Walk on the Other Side

gives herself freely to her man. This is that moment when that woman rises high above the heavens and just as she is about to touch that far away cloud he pulls her back so that her moment will last just a little longer. At that moment its at test, yes a test and you don't know weather to scream or just to be quiet and enjoy this moment because it will only last for a short time a brief moment in time when it seems as if the entire world just stops, just for you and he has created this moment just for you and trust me I am loving every second, I mean every second and anticipating what each second will bring me. I know that each second will be filled with extreme pleasure, this I truly believe because that is all that you have delivered on this day. Just when I thought I had reached the point of no return it happened. You reached down and lifted my head so gently whispered nothing but how much you were enjoying taking me to unknown places, and at that

A Walk on the Other Side

moment all that I had was released
like a waterfall and then you knew
how much I enjoyed you also just
from a simple whisper...

This Picture

This picture was taken for you, while thinking of you being in me, where you and I long for you to be. The nights are long and the days are longer, just thinking about being with you, yet being without you has a burning so deep in my soul that the word fire means nothing.... being with you that moment and only that moment will calm this inferno desire that has been growing in my lions for you...

I say to you my sweet sexy man, come to me now and come quickly because I feel the wetness coming down my leg and I don't want this explosion to happen without you so please my dear come before I explode with all my desire, come quickly...

Yes, I have been holding all of this sweet essence just for you, I'm holding on with all that I have but at this moment I'm thinking of you, about you being in me and... I'm about to explode and the juices that are coming from my golden paradise shouldn't be wasted !!!

So please come to me...

Come quickly...

Tomorrow

You say want to live for tomorrow,
so you have to start living today.
You say you want unconditional love
tomorrow,
but what happened today. You say
you are looking for your tomorrow ,
but you have to let go of yesterday.
Take my
hand and we will explore the endless
possibilities of what tomorrow holds,
let's see, feel and taste the essence of
the sweetness of joy that awaits you,
at the dawn of tomorrow
Tomorrow will come, and it will
hold all of your deepest desires,
unconditional love, peace within
your soul and
endless days and nights of happiness
that you have longed for, but you
must to let go of yesterday.
Come, take my hand we are at the
dawn of tomorrow, but first you have
let go of the hurt, the pain, and yes
you may
have cry a few tears, and your heart
may hurt. Please don't be afraid I
will be here to wipe your tears and
mend your

A Walk on the Other Side

heart, for I am tomorrow, and I have
been waiting for you.
I have that unconditional love that's
you have been longing for, I have the
peace that will reach down into the
parts
of your soul you never knew existed,
I will not hurt you, and I'm here your
tomorrow and I have been waiting
just for
you...Rest here in my heart; as I
cultivate your mind, body an soul, so
you will be ready for all that
tomorrow has in
store for you
I'm open, so come in and be
saturated with endless love which
will empower you to have endless
tomorrows far
beyond what your dreams or
imagination. Believe and see that
tomorrow is really here, for
yesterday is gone and
we are about to embark on a journey
that is full of all that you have
yearned for, come look and see for
tomorrow is
here; it's on the horizon. So now its
time to take our first steps into
tomorrow with our eyes wide open
hand in

A Walk on the Other Side

hand. As we walk into tomorrow, we
stop and realize we have but one
regret…we waited too long to let go
of
yesterday.

Urban Cowboy

Would you, can you come through
because right now I need a good
some good down home loving
tonight...I need to grab the sheets and
scream your name, grab your ass,
wrap my legs around your neck
while I cum multiple times. Yea, I
like to moan but it's been a while and
momma needs you to come through
and do some damage to this
midsection.

I need to be flipped, dipped, slapped
on this ass so I can remember who
Daddy is in this bedroom. Yea, don't
play you know you want to come
through so you can have a double dip
of cream dripping all over that lovely
shaft.

Yea, and don't forget that we like to
go for rides into the sunset, oh shit
where's the horse that would be you
Daddy and I still have my hat and I

A Walk on the Other Side

have my boots on now all I need is
my Urban Cowboy so let's get this
session started because I have an
excess juices that are waiting for you
so come now...come
quickly...come...come...come....so
we can cum and cum... All night
long...

When

When will I...When can I...How can
I feel the warmth of your love come
down on me....There is no reason to
wait...There is no reason be   patient
anymore...There has been a shift is
the wind and I need to feel you and I
mean all of you, from head to toe.

I need you to consume me totally
with your mind as well as your body
while you get ready to take what
belongs to you...Can you cover me
with your love, without leaving
anything to question if so tell me
when will I , how can I feel your
warmth come down all over me.

When can I feel your warm shaft
gliding pass my thighs, entering my
already moist gateway paradise,
making me reach up to grab and pull
you even closer so that I can make
sure that I get every single inch of
you inside of me so that this fire can
be slightly extinguished, because it

will never go completely out.

When will I be able to lock my legs
around you as we go into orgasmic
convulsions together after you have
consumed my body into yours and I
have succumbed to your every will
as you have desired me too.

Oh my not done yet, another round
there is one thing I forgot...I want to
flip over so that you can cover my
entire front and back with your love,
and we shall leave nothing
undiscovered for this love thing is
eternal and everlasting and we shall
discover new and exciting ways to
please each other in ways that we
both will be amazed, so now we have
no reason to wait, and no reason to
go against the shift of the wind...let's
just feel the warmth of our love come
down slowly and enjoy the shift in
the wind that allows our love to
flow...

A Walk on the Other Side

YOUR VOICE

When I hear your voice something goes through me like never before. I go, oh, my what has come over me and it's your voice. Yes, your voice sends me into a world of sensual feelings that have been sleep, but now they are awake and longing for more. Just to hear your voice it saturates my being as it causes me to saturate my bed as I lay talking and listening to you, but wanting and longing for you to be here with me, and in me making me feel the things that will take me to another realm of sensual bliss, for the pleasure would be mine to release what I have stored up for this very moment. Yes, your voice will make me melt like butter and come to a complete stop as you begin to enter my gateway to heaven, that will be waiting with anticipation, wet, hot and just waiting for you to enter with your lovely dark shaft that will release all that I have stored up just for this moment. Wait, stop don't move let me look at what I'm about to get, better yet come closer and let me have just a taste of pure dark chocolate before I release what I have stored up just for this moment. Mmmmm, just as I imagined lovely, tasty, and just so dam good enough to eat all night, but right now I'm ready, oh so ready to release what I have stored up just for this moment, all I need is for you to say one word because it's your voice that has me ready to spin endlessly into the abyss of sexual desires. Yes, I like that whisper that in my ear again just as you enter and I promise you the ride will be endless. Yes, oh my yes, you have crossed over into my gateway and I can't breath, I can't speak I just want to release what I have stored up for this moment. Here I go and with that I grabbed you tighter as you spoke to my body without speaking and while you whispered in my ear to let it go and I was done...I

A Walk on the Other Side

released and you released and now I
am ready to hear your voice again,
because I have more stored up just
for you for future moments.

Fantasy 'n

Fairytales

A Walk on the Other Side

The Dick Pleasing Man

Do you know the pleasing dick man... the pleasing dick man?

Do you know the pleasing dick man, my pussy needs him fast.

I want to find the pleasing dick man. the pleasing dick man, I need him really bad.

Help me find the pleasing dick man, I really need to feel it. My pussy will super grip it.

Horny as can be, please come and help me.

If you know the pleasing dick man, find him as fast as you can.

Hickory Dickory Cock

Hickory Dickory Dock

My hot twat ran up the clock

The clock struck one

His cock went hard

Oh my...

Hickory Dickory Cock

Little Miss Muffet

Little Miss Muffet

sat on her pussy

sucking the hell out of

that big dick flex...

Along came a spider,

sat down beside her

and said ...

damn Miss Muffet

can I be next...

Patty Cake

Patty cake patty cake dick in hand

Put it in my oven has fast as you can

Bang it bang it as hard as you can

Yes daddy make me cum all over this man

Slap my ass with them big old hands

Thrust it one more time my Mandingo Man

Now just bang it bang it daddy just like that

Patty cake patty cake dick in hand

Keep it in my oven as long as you can

I just need to cum all over this man...

A Walk on the Other Side

Star Light

Star light, star bright,

First dick I see tonight...

I wish I may, I wish I might

Ride upon this dick all
freakin night...

The End

About the Author

Tina was born in Yonkers, NY and educated in the New York School System. After graduation from high school, she attended The College of Charleston, SC with a major in Criminal Justice and a minor in Communications. Tina returned to New York where she continued her education and received a degree in Communications. Tina has been writing for many years.

Overall, nothing gives her more joy than writing at this point in her life. Tina lived in Florida for a number of years and was known locally as a writer of many gospel plays such as: **Deception, Some Kind Of Christmas, What Is Easter All About, The Pageant,** and **Those People**, just to name a few.

Tina has a website dedicated to her poetry, where she clearly embraces the gift that is within her; the gift of poetry, the ability to tell a story through words.

Tina has been writing plays for **SoReal Productions** with director *Chris Scott* since 1998. It is a life long commitment between the two of them to continue to bring words to life through the arts and continue to bless people with their talents.

Tina has three wonderful children who support her in all of her endeavors, along with her loving family.

Tina Wright aka The Quiet Poet

A Walk on the Other Side

Made in the USA
Las Vegas, NV
07 February 2022